An Allegheny National Forest Adventure

The Mystery of the Wailing Woods

DIANE KLEIN
& TIM KNIGHT

Across the Pond Publications

ISBN: 978-0-578-82840-4

Published in the United States of America by

Across the Pond Publications
PO Box 14132
Pittsburgh, PA 15239

acrossthepondpublications.com

Dedication

<u>Diane Klein</u>

To my children, Korie and Scott Klein, who always were and always will be the BEST fiction and nonfiction storytellers, ever!

<u>Tim Knight</u>

My first dedication is to my own Mum, with whom I would share long walks as a child, during which we would both create elaborate stories set in the countryside through which we walked, and with whom I would also play delightfully silly and intricate word games. My second dedication is to my own children, Rachel, Jess, and James, who are the best things that I have ever had a share in creating. Finally, a dedication to all the children whom I have taught, who encouraged me in my storytelling, even if it was just a way of them avoiding having to do some work!

Acknowledgments

Many thanks to our young first-draft readers: Anne, Bella, Cole, Desi, Eliza, Kyle (mom-Deanna), and Talia, who provided us with the essential feedback needed to make this story come alive. Thanks also to the many anonymous children in the neighborhood who helped us select the cover design. Additional thanks to Scott Klein for his technical assistance and the fine residents of Kane, PA, and the forest rangers in the Allegheny National Forest for their willingness to share the information and beauty of this special place.

Contents

Prologue

The Allegheny National Forest is a beautiful area in the northwestern section of Pennsylvania. Verdant beyond what your eyes might believe, the multi-layered hues of green and gold make a perfect place to run, play, hike, and explore. It also has many hidden secrets... and that is where our story begins...

Chapter 1: Griffin and Caleigh

Griffin McGee ran excitedly over to his neighbor's house. It was only a few houses down from his own home, but on hiking days it felt like a mile away. Up the wooden steps he galloped, taking them two at a time. Screeching to a stop just before running headfirst into the bright red front door, he raised his fist to pound on the door when it suddenly swung open wide. Standing there, hands balled at her waist, feet spread in a warrior stance, was Caleigh Providence. She scanned Griffin from head to toe and scowled.

"Where is your gear?" she demanded with her usual authority. Caleigh, Griffin's best friend since forever, was a straight-talking girl, and it was clear from her facial expressions and her tone of voice that she was not pleased with Griffin's appearance.

Griffin grinned. She sounded tough, but Caleigh was also the first person to jump to his side if he needed a buddy, so he never let her tone sway him. He rather enjoyed it.

"Ummm, I thought we could work on my gear together. You kind of always have in mind what you think I should be wearing when we go hiking," Griffin responded with a smirk. He knew exactly how to get Caleigh riled up and he just loved doing that to her. It made for so much fun when they did get out hiking in the woods.

Caleigh and Griffin were friends from the moment they met each other as one-year-old toddlers. They went to the same preschool and now the same primary school. They took all the same classes in school and enjoyed many of the same outdoor sports. They were an interesting pair. Griffin was tall and built for sports, making him look a bit older than his 10 years. His dark wavy brown hair and eyes came from his mother's side of the family, not his Irish dad's. Caleigh, on the other hand, was short and petite. Her long auburn hair and gold-flecked eyes gave her a rather impish appearance, a near twin of her mother. She loved many of the winter sports that were popular in northern Pennsylvania. These two became fast friends and were quite sure they ruled their world in the small town of Kane, Pennsylvania.

Kane was nestled nearly in the center of the Allegheny National Forest, a place a great beauty and lots of fantastic hiding places and cool secrets. Everyone in Kane adored the ANF (what the locals called the forest), and Caleigh and Griffin loved hiking every single Saturday along the trails of their magical weekend retreat. To them, it truly felt like a wonderland. Any child would love to run free in this forest where your imagination could go wild! Who wouldn't like to paddle down cool streams that turned and twisted, from deep shaded pools beneath the hemlocks to sunlit waters that flowed leisurely through the tall fir glades? And who would turn down the chance to climb? Finding your way up a thick trunk to the limbs of one of the tallest living things on Earth was just plain exciting. Imagine the fun if for just for a moment, you could pretend to be one of the many creatures in the forest, from the tiniest boring beetle in a tree's bark to the mightiest eagle that made its home on the top branches of the trees?

Oh, yes, the ANF was a very magical place, so it was no surprise that Caleigh and Griffin loved to spend their weekends exploring this forest.

Caleigh grabbed Griffin's hand and marched him back to his house and up the front steps. Sitting on a wooden Adirondack porch chair was Tom McGee, Griffin's dad. He looked up, startled at the clomping sounds in front of him. Mr. McGee was the local newspaper's photojournalist. He also had an interest in all things strange and mystical, collecting unique objects and photographing unusual things in nature. When he drove the kids to their hiking site, he often accompanied them on their adventures, snapping pictures along the way. He always laughed at the sight of his son being instructed by their feisty neighbor. Now, he lowered the newspaper to speak to the children.

"Good morning, you two! Caleigh, you look like you are on a mission, dragging Griffin up the steps that way! What's going on? Where are we headed today?"

Caleigh giggled. "It's a great morning, Mr. McGee! Griffin and I are heading straight into the forest at Rimrock Trail for our weekly hunt, but he doesn't have the gear he needs. I figured I would come over and set him straight before we head out and you drop us off."

Griffin grinned and rolled his eyes at his dad, who smiled back and shot him a quick wink. Yes, his dad knew that Griffin did these kinds of things on purpose to tease Caleigh. That's what friends do!

Caleigh pulled on Griffin's hand and said, "C'mon already, Griff. Let's head in, get your gear and some water, and head out to the trails.".

Chapter 2: The Orb

With that, they bounded right through the front door and nearly tripped up the steps to his room. And what a room it was! Griffin loved the outdoors just as much as Caleigh, and his room overflowed with amazing bits and pieces of the outside from their previous excursions. Caleigh scanned the room with a smile. Every wall was covered with artifacts from their forest adventures. Hanging gracefully on the wall over Griffin's bed, like a bough from one of the millions of fir trees in the ANF, were several branches loaded with pinecones. There were hundreds of cones in all sizes, shapes, and colors. And the smell! Oh, it was delicious, just like being out in the forest. Another wall was decorated with tons of pictures that he took each week. Everything from birds, to butterflies, to gurgling brooks and fish were displayed in brilliant color. Caleigh's favorite wall, though, was the one behind his desk. Griffin was allowed to draw and paint on that wall. It was beautiful! He drew the imaginary and legendary creatures that they had talked and read about during their adventures and hoped to encounter one day.

Griffin got his backpack out of his closet and turned to look at Caleigh, waiting for her directions, as she always had to tell him exactly what she wanted him to bring along. But Caleigh wasn't looking at Griffin. She was staring at his desk. Slowly, she walked over to the furniture and leaned down carefully to look at a glowing orb that was perched in a stand on the corner of the surface. She turned her head and with a quizzical expression on her face she softly said, "What is THAT, Griffin? It is magical!!!"

Griffin ambled up beside her and whispered, "Yes, it really is amazing, isn't it? I couldn't wait for you to see it! You know how my dad loves to collect things that are all mysterious and strange? Well, he said just the other day someone left it on his desk at work and when nobody claimed it by yesterday, he brought it home for me. It's almost like a crystal ball. Look into the middle, you can practically see things!"

Caleigh and Griffin leaned over to look into the center of the orb. Both gasped as it began to glow. "Did you see that?" they said simultaneously.

As they gazed into the orb, their eyes widened with astonishment. How could this be? There were streams and rafts and fish and bugs! The stream they saw was not something small and insignificant — no, it was a mighty river to be explored. Then they saw themselves launch rafts made from the dried reeds that they gathered from the side of the stream.

They shook their heads in disbelief, and then they looked deeper into the center. There, they saw themselves standing on board the rafts along with a crew of fellow explorers venturing somewhere entirely new. Where the stream became shallow and seemed to dance between glittering pebbles, they suddenly saw wild rapids that could claim the lives of everyone on the rafts at any moment. Then the stream turned sharply. Its bank formed a deep pool where the fish seemed to bask and leap at the winged dragonfly insects that hovered in the shafts of light.

Caleigh and Griffin saw a mysterious city that was new and strange and exotic to them; somewhere where the mythical Golden Fleece and its guardian the Hydra could be. The fish in the pool now looked like great glittering sea monsters that could, in one mouthful, seize the ships of unwary travelers. Before those explorers could react, the huge fish could drag them to the depths of the raging waters, to be devoured at leisure.

Caleigh and Griffin slowly turned and looked at each other in awe. Had the orb predicted their adventurous future? What a brilliant time they were going to have today in their forest!

Chapter 3: The Forest

Mr. McGee dropped the children off at the trailhead for their favorite trail and reminded them to be safe and call him on their cell phone when they were finished hiking. The pair of friends stood together, tingling with excitement, at the entrance of Rimrock Trail. There was always something special about walking up to a trailhead entrance of the ANF. Standing under the towering evergreen and deciduous trees, you felt as tiny as a fairy. The earth was so rich and nourishing for the lush growth that you could actually smell the dirt. With each step, the warm mellow earthy scent drifted around you and made you feel like you belonged; like you, too, were a part of nature. As they paused, considering the multiple forks in front of them, Griffin practically chirped, "Which path today then, Caleigh?"

Caleigh thought for a moment and said, "Let's leave it up to fate. I'll toss a coin; heads, we take the far right-hand path and tails, we take the far left-hand one."

She took a coin from her pocket and spun it into the air. It glittered like a jewel in the autumn sunlight as it rose up into the sky and fell back down, to be caught deftly in Caleigh's upturned palm.

"And?" inquired Griffin.

Caleigh smiled, returned the coin to her pocket, and took the right-hand path, which followed a small stream deep into the woods. Griffin ran to catch up to her, tagged her with his hand, and yelled, "Bet you can't catch me!" He sped past his friend down the path with all the agility of a mountain lion. Caleigh needed no encouraging and chased her friend, dodging branches and leaping over fallen logs as they headed deeper and deeper into the forest. They slowed to a trot as they approached the old wooden slat bridge crossing a deep chasm. It was a bit scary and rickety, and Caleigh and Griffin held each other's hands as they neared the bridge. One behind the other, they carefully treaded across the boards and then burst back into a full gallop as they ran further into their forest.

Now, Caleigh and Griffin thought that they knew every inch of the forest, particularly this trail, even though sometimes they would pretend to be lost, as that was a most thrilling game — provided, of course, that they weren't lost for real. So, it was to their surprise that the pair came to a halt in a clearing that neither recognized. The air was still and the sun warm upon their backs. In the center of the clearing was a pool that looked just like one of the images they had seen in the magic orb that Griffin's dad had given him. The children were thirsty after their run, so they took a sip from the clear pool. They were shocked to find that instead of tasting fresh, the water tasted slightly salty, as if it were full of tears!

Even more surprising, the grass on one side of the pool seemed to have been trampled by some large creature and the grass itself looked frozen as if it was winter and not a balmy autumn day. Griffin investigated what looked like crystals of ice on the grass. He crouched down and lightly rubbed his hand over the blades of grass. They felt stiff to his touch rather than soft and pliable.

"How strange this is," muttered Griffin under his breath and knelt down even closer to the ground to get a better look. Caleigh was watching intently from the other side of the pool and got up on her tiptoes to try to peer over in Griffin's direction.

"What in the heck is he staring at?" She shook her head quizzically and began moving in his direction to see for herself.

"WAIT!" Griffin shouted, holding out his palm to stop her in her tracks. "Wait a minute. This is just so strange. I have to get some pictures to show my dad, so you can't come over here and trample all over the scene."

Caleigh was indignant. "Trample all over the scene! Who do you think you are talking to, Griffin McGee? I am not some dumb little polliwog. I know to be careful and I want to see what you are looking at!" With that, Caleigh gingerly walked around the opposite end of the pool to come up on the area that Griffin was cautiously protecting. She saw immediately the different colors in the grass as well as the smashed appearance and she, too, got down on her knees for a closer look. Then she stuck her nose right in the middle of the grass, closed her eyes, and took a big smell.

"Well, it doesn't smell any different than other grass. I guess that is kind of good."

Griffin stared at her in amazement; was she actually smelling the grass? Really? Then he nearly dropped his camera when Caleigh reached out and grabbed several blades of grass and popped them in her mouth.

"Are you crazy?" Griffin shouted. "You have no idea what this is all about and you put that in your mouth?!"

Caleigh smirked and started to cough. "HACK, HACK, HACK."

Then she widened her eyes in surprise and covered her mouth as though she was about to be ill, still smirking behind her hands.

Griffin charged over to Caleigh with his water bottle, unscrewing the lid as he thrust the bottle in her direction. He shouted, "Here, drink this immediately! Wash out your mouth!"

Caleigh rolled on her back, laughing with glee. "It's just salty-tasting, Griffin, nothing more. Really, I AM OK!"

Griffin stared at her in disbelief. What a rotten trick to play on him. He would have to figure a way to even the score. In the meantime, he stood up, yanked back his water bottle, reapplied the lid, scowled in her direction, and started to walk back to where he had been to take those pictures.

"Last time I help you when you are hacking up a lung!" he grumbled loudly. "Now, let's get some pictures to try to figure out what this is all about. Why are there crystals of salt on this grass?"

At that moment, a gentle breeze came up and the grass began to sway gently, back and forth, back and forth. Then the branches of the trees surrounding the clearing joined in the dance as well. As they swayed, they sounded as if they were sighing with regret, knowing that it would soon be winter and they would lose their grip on the golden leaves that they wore with such pride. It was a sad sound but also a beautiful one. Griffin and Caleigh paused to listen, lost for a moment in the hypnotic sound, and they recalled a scene they had witnessed in the magical orb. Again, the images caught them off guard and they found themselves staring at each other, unaware of time passing. It felt like they had all the time in the world to just stand and listen to the woods.

Then the breeze died down and the sound faded into the tree canopy. Caleigh and Griffin rapidly shook their heads, clearing their minds of the mesmerizing haze.

Chapter 4: The Creature

"Shhhheeeesh, that was weird!" Griffin exclaimed. Caleigh slowly nodded in agreement, her brow furrowed.

Griffin readied his camera and prepared to take photographs of the trampled grass and its mysterious salty crystal coat, for he knew that none of the adults at home would believe their story otherwise. At that moment, the strangest thing of this whole strange day took place. A wail, incredibly low, soft, and sad, drifted from the trees beyond. Now, the wind had already died down and the tree branches had given up their dance and returned to stillness. So had their slender cousins, the grasses. How, then, could Griffin and Caleigh explain the sighing, sad, beautiful sound that had suddenly arisen? The children turned to each other; this was no random sound of nature but music instead. It had a melody and even words, though they were words that neither Griffin nor Caleigh could grasp.

"We HAVE to check this out, Griff!" Caleigh whispered while moving in the direction of the sounds. Cautiously, with the smallest, quietest footsteps possible, they crept along the grass-covered path toward the moaning sounds. They kept shifting their gaze right, then left, to try to catch a glimpse of whatever was making this intriguing sound.

Griffin took the lead and they walked for what felt like an eternity along the heavily overgrown trail, listening intently to the soft wailing, until they reached a small, deeply shaded grove. Griffin gingerly pulled aside the low hanging branches of the conifer trees. He gasped. Caleigh watched his face intently. She saw his jaw drop practically to the ground.

"What do you see?" she hissed under her breath.

Griffin moved at a snail's pace and nudged the branches further aside, taking great pains not to make any noises at all. There, before their eyes, was a small hairy creature, hunched over a little pond, holding a tiny frog, and the creature was crying!

Shocked, Caleigh moved forward ever so slightly. Griffin pressed her hand into his, gently restraining her from moving any more. Hands linked, they looked at each other; eyes glassy with amazement signaled that now was not the time for words. Now was the time just to be still and observant, savoring a moment that they would remember forever.

The frog sat in the creature's hand and gently swayed in time with the rhythm of the sobbing as if here, despite the sadness, it felt accepted and safe. Occasionally, the tiny frog produced a quiet gentle chirrup of its own as if it were playing a part in this soulful duet. Incredibly, each time the frog chirruped, the creature smiled ever so slightly and stroked its tiny companion's back.

Griffin noticed that beneath the creature's thin hair was what looked like a warty skin, "more like a toad's than a frog's," he thought. Even more remarkable were the creature's eyes, which were the same sumptuous golden color as the polished agate in Griffin's father's precious mineral collection.

"Imagine," Griffin thought, "to be as ugly as this creature was but to have just one thing of such beauty."

Unbeknownst to the two, the creature had sensed it was being observed. It moved its head only the tiniest bit to the side, paused, sighed, and smiled a secret smile.

Time seemed to stand still for Griffin and Caleigh as they watched the curious scene. The little creature lowered its hands toward the pond, and the frog, after one final chirrup, jumped with a gentle plop back into the water. As far as they could tell, the hairy creature had apparently not noticed Caleigh and Griffin hidden in the shrubs. With careful, almost silent, footsteps, the creature stepped onto a path that led even farther into the forest. The ferns unfurled behind him and within moments it was as if he had never been there at all.

Chapter 5: X Marks the Spot

For several minutes neither child said anything. All that could be heard was the gentle autumn breeze and the melodic chirruping of the frog that had sat so contentedly in the creature's outstretched hand. It now rested, with the same air of contentment, in the shallow water at the edge of the pool, where the water was cool and the light dappled by overhanging trees.

Now it was time for words, lots of words! Caleigh spoke first. "We must come here again, so we can see whatever it was that we just saw AGAIN."

Griffin nodded rapidly in instant agreement and spoke just as quickly. "I have no idea what it was that we saw, but it was amazing. I mean, it was small and kind of ugly-looking, but it was so gentle! When we get home, we have to look this up. I so wanted to take a picture but I didn't dare move an inch or it might have been frightened off."

Griffin and Caleigh paused to reflect for a moment. Then she blurted, "Let's mark the pond so we know where to return." She knew that whatever she used to mark the location would have to be both permanent and distinctive, and she had noticed just the thing close by. At the side of the pool was a particularly smooth chunk of pink granite that was almost perfectly spherical. Caleigh dug a hole in the soft earth with her hands and then rummaged in her pockets for something of hers that could be buried beneath the sphere. She found one of her good luck pieces, a small figurine of Alice in Wonderland; it was one of her most precious possessions. Griffin grasped Caleigh's idea and from inside his coat pocket he brought out a magnifying glass that could be used to examine minerals or the tiny beasts that belonged in this mesmerizing place. Both put their special objects deep in the hole and carefully placed the pink granite sphere on top to stand guard.

They stood, wiped the dirt off their hands, and turned in a small circle, making sure to take close note of any additional landmarks that would help them return to this site. At that moment Griffin smacked himself on his forehead. "What is wrong with me?" he exclaimed. "I have my camera. I can take all the pictures we need to find this place again."

Caleigh rolled her eyes at Griffin and laughed loud and long, agreeing that taking pictures would, indeed, provide a speedy solution.

As they hiked back down toward the regular trail, Griffin took pictures of uniquely shaped tree trunks and large moss- and lichen-covered rock formations. He didn't want to mark the path in any way that was harmful to the forest, so only pictures would do. Caleigh had a particularly good eye for spotting these landmarks, making Griffin's job easy.

Finally, they found themselves back on the main trail and headed toward the trailhead where they were to call Mr. McGee for their ride home. You can imagine their surprise when they arrived at the entrance and were met not only by Mr. McGee, but by an ANF forest ranger officer as well.

Chapter 6: Consequences

Griffin had been speed walking into the parking lot, working out in his mind how he was going to tell his dad about the creature, when he pulled up short and stopped abruptly. He stood rock solid, looking at the two rather stern adults in front of him. Caleigh, who had been walking head down in deep thought, didn't see him stop and crashed right into him, practically knocking Griffin to the ground.

"What the heck, Griffin. Why did you stop like that?" Then Caleigh saw the reason and suddenly became much less assertive, looking back and forth between the two men with some anxiety.

Mr. McGee at first looked angry, but then his facial expression turned to relief. "Do you two have any idea what time it is? Do you know how worried I was when you hadn't called at least an hour ago?"

Ranger Oakes also looked concerned and added, "Your father called the ranger station an hour ago when he hadn't heard from you. I met him here and we were about to set out in search for you both. That's a serious thing, for us to have to search for you."

All of the excitement that Griffin and Caleigh felt after their incredible hike was now as deflated as a flat bicycle tire. They wanted to tell Mr. McGee all about the creature, but kept quiet while the adults scolded them.

Finally, when there was a break in the adult side of the discussion, Griffin spoke up. "We never looked at our watches, Dad. We had no idea what time it was and lost track of the time because we were having such an amazing adventure today. We really want to tell you the whole story, but maybe this isn't the time to do that."

Mr. McGee and Ranger Oakes briefly looked at each other and then back at the children. Ranger Oakes spoke first.

"Do you understand how critical it is for you to be aware of the time and your surroundings when you go hiking? There are so many dangers in the forest, and I know you think you are really excellent hikers, but you are kids and you need to be much more careful if you are to continue your Saturday hikes. Do you understand that?"

Next, it was Mr. McGee's turn. "Griffin, I know that you and Caleigh so very much love your hiking adventures, but, you two have to PROMISE me that you will NEVER lose track of time like this again. You two frightened all of us. Caleigh, your mom and dad were just frantic that I hadn't heard from you!"

Caleigh and Griffin hung their heads in shame and nodded that they understood what the ranger and Mr. McGee had said. Caleigh's eyes were brimming with tears and she whispered, "I am so, so sorry, Mr. McGee. We didn't want to scare anybody. I promise to never do this again, ever."

Griffin had a lump in his throat the size of a baseball and could barely swallow, let alone talk, but he also knew that he better say something if he was ever to be permitted to hike the forest with Caleigh again.

"I am really sorry, Dad and Ranger Oakes. I take the blame because I was supposed to watch the time and call. I promise both of you with all my heart that I'll never scare you again like this and will always watch the time. I PROMISE."

With that, Ranger Oakes patted both children on the back and thanked them for listening to him and for their oath to be more careful when hiking. He climbed into his Jeep and headed back to the ranger station.

Mr. McGee heaved a big sigh and said, "OK, guys. Get into the car and let me call your folks, Caleigh, so they know you are safe and sound. Then I will call Mom, Griffin, to put her mind at ease too."

They all climbed into the car and once their seatbelts were fastened, Mr. McGee turned to face the children in the back and said, "I want to also thank you for listening to us, not arguing, and promising to do better when you go out hiking. Now, tell me about that story!"

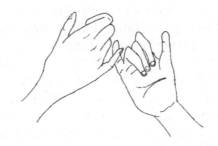

Chapter 7: The Almost Story

Now, Griffin had a reputation for being truthful and it was one for which he was rightly proud, but what really happened had been so fantastic that he felt he couldn't possibly tell it. What if the adults thought that what really happened was a lie and that he had made up such a far-fetched tale to get Caleigh and him out of trouble? Then again, and far worse, what if they did believe him? Wouldn't the forest be full of people trying to track down what they had seen? The creature had seemed sad enough when it was alone — just imagine its terror if it felt that it was being hunted.

Griffin quickly squeezed Caleigh's hand and hoped that the telepathy of friendship would lead her, with no words exchanged, to understand why he was not about to tell his father the whole truth.

"We thought we heard something strange, Dad, and I was curious, you know how I am about science — so I said to Caleigh that we should try to find out what it was, but we ended up getting deeper and deeper into the forest until we were lost."

Caleigh's eyelids flickered but she said nothing and hoped that she would be spared cross-examination by Mr. McGee. Mr. McGee shrugged and said that he hoped that they had both learned their lesson. To which both children nodded uncomfortably. The rest of the journey home was largely conducted in an awkward silence, as was supper, and Griffin was glad when it was time for him to go to bed.

He found it difficult to sleep, consumed as he was with the lie that he had told but also with what he and Caleigh had actually seen. They had witnessed something with their own eyes that belonged in a fairy tale. Eventually, sleep took him and it was if the whole night he heard the song that they had heard in the glade in the forest. When he opened his hand, within the fingers was not a frog, as with the creature, but Caleigh. Griffin awoke with a sadness that had never touched him before. This vivid vision startled him completely. He knew that dreams sometimes seemed like a peek into the future. Was this strange dream some sort of premonition?

Chapter 8: Trust

The following day, the McGees were going to visit Griffin's grandparents. Griffin always looked forward to these days, as his grandparents were masters at staying on the right side of the line between treating and spoiling their beloved grandchildren. Their proper English-style garden, which Griffin loved to play in, was a little wild and overgrown and full of secret paths, the scent of flowers, and the hum of contented insects. In the center of the garden was a pond which, like the rest of their garden, teemed with life and on whose surface floated translucent globes of the darkest green. If you held the globes up to your eyes, it was as if there was a whole green world inside of them. Griffin would imagine what creatures might live in its depths.

But when the McGees' car pulled up outside of his grandparents' house, rain was beating upon the windows and it was clear that there would be no playing in the garden today. Griffin wasn't too disappointed that he couldn't play outside because having to stay in would mean he could explore his grandparents' book collection. He hoped that there might be, buried deep inside the pages of one of them, a clue to the identity of the mysterious beast that he and Caleigh had seen in the forest. Griffin had good reason to suspect the existence of such a book; one rainy day in the past, he had discovered a green tome called On the Track of Unknown Animals. Griffin, trusting as he was, suspected that the photograph of the Tatzelwurm from the Alps pictured at the beginning of the book had, in fact, been fabricated from a cigar tube and a set of cardboard teeth. This, however, was not the only book on unusual animals. There were books on sea serpents and the Sasquatch too; maybe there might be something similar on sad, strange animals of Pennsylvania.

Gram called him into the dining room for one of her family's old traditions, homemade cake and tea that was poured out of a teapot covered with a knitted coat. His gram's British family background seeped into everything she did, and Griffin loved every second, even the extra cuddles that she and Grandpa bestowed on him at each visit. After a bit of conversation, Griffin asked to be excused so that he could explore their library.

Griffin began to search the shelves. After only a few minutes he found a book with the title Fearsome Creatures of the Lumberwoods, with a Few Desert and Mountain Beasts. The book was dusty and looked as if it hadn't been opened since it was published in 1910, but perhaps the answers he wanted were inside those pages. Griffin slowly thumbed through the yellowed pages, examining each picture.

There was a whole catalogue of incredible beasts, starting with the Wapaloosie, which could climb the tallest of trees and retained the ability to do that even when it had been turned into a pair of mittens. The

Slide Rock Bolter was a gigantic creature with no legs but two claws instead, which it used to pull itself up mountains. There it would wait for unwary passers-by who would then be gobbled up by the beast as it rolled down the slope — jaws first!

And then Griffin found what he was looking for, a creature from the forests of Pennsylvania that was so sad that it wept continually on account of its ill-fitting warty skin. Once a hunter had caught one and put the creature in a sack. Understandably, the poor creature wailed for the entire journey back to the hunter's lodge. But when he arrived home to check his ill-gotten gains, there was nothing left in his sack but a pool of bubbles.

Griffin was so busy reading that he hadn't noticed his grandfather come into the room. He almost jumped out of his own skin when he felt a hand on his shoulder.

"Have you found anything interesting, son?" his grandpa asked.

Griffin looked up and said, "Grandpa, do you think there is a possibility that any of these creatures are real?"

Grandpa looked at Griffin wide-eyed and his big blue eyes twinkled with glee. An ear-to-ear grin spread across his face as he raised his hand to his chin, rhythmically twirling his soft short white beard. He began to nod his head slowly.

"You know, Griffin, I am a big believer in the strange and unaccountable. I wouldn't be the least bit surprised if some of these strange beasties did, at some point, exist. After all, most stories, even fairy tales, do have a speck of truth. Every country around the world seems to have these wonderful stories about some sort of amazing creature. Wouldn't it be kind of cool if someone found one of them now? Just imagine how incredible that discovery might be!" Grandpa chuckled out loud at this thought.

Griffin stared at his grandpa, debating frantically whether he should tell him about what he and Caleigh had seen in the forest.

Grandpa was watching Griffin's reaction closely. Normally, the boy would be jumping up and down, begging to hear some of the fantastic tales he had to share, but not today.

"Hmmmmm," he thought, "something is up here." Out loud, he said, "You seem to be thinking really hard about something, Griff. Is there something on your mind you want to discuss?"

Grandpa pulled up his favorite chair and sat down directly across from Griffin. Griffin shifted uncomfortably in his own chair and actually broke out in a sweat. Small drops of moisture gathered on his forehead, and Griffin took a quick swipe at them, hoping that Grandpa wouldn't notice his nerves.

Griffin's mind was racing. Grandpa was a really great guy. He could always be trusted with a secret. He proved that when he kept a big birthday surprise party secret from Grandma for months. And now, Grandpa confided that he believed the creatures could exist. He even said that he thought it would be great to find one alive now.

Decision made. Griffin cleared his throat and said, "I have a secret and I mean a really, REALLY HUGE secret that, if I tell you, you have to promise with all your heart that you will keep it a secret too."

Grandpa could not remember the last time he had seen such a serious look on his grandson's face, and the tone of his voice made it clear that Griffin felt very strongly about what he might tell him. "Griffin, if you want to tell me something that special, I will keep it a secret unless it is something that can hurt you. So, you decide if you want to share your secret with me. I'll understand if you decide not to share. Although I must say, you have my curiosity radar up now!"

Griffin took a big gulp of air and decided he would tell Grandpa a part of the secret and see how he reacted before telling him everything.

"OK, Grandpa. I'm glad you are sitting down because this is a pretty amazing story." Griffin went on to tell Grandpa about the hike he and Caleigh had taken yesterday and that they had wandered deeper along a trail than they were used to. They had found this area of grass that was so strange because it had white crystals all over it. He told Grandpa about Caleigh tasting it and reporting that it was salty. He continued to describe the strange wind and then the sound, a crying-like sound.

Griffin watched Grandpa closely for a reaction. Would Grandpa make fun of the story? Would he be curious about what made the sound? Would he be worried that they went too far into the forest?

Grandpa listened closely to every word. When Griffin suddenly stopped talking, he peered at him and said, "Is there more to this story? I believe you heard a strange sound. I have been in the forest many times and have heard the wind whistle through the trees. It often sounds like a song and I just imagine it could sound like a wailing cry."

Griffin was relieved and excited. Grandpa got it! "Yes, there is more," said Griffin. "We went to look for the sound and saw something. No kidding, Grandpa! We don't know what we saw, but we saw something that was crying. And suddenly, it stopped crying and disappeared into the forest. I have to tell you, though; I did NOT tell Dad. I was afraid that he might think we were lying to get out of trouble for being late. And Caleigh has not breathed a word of it to anyone. I remembered that you had all these wonderful books here about creatures, so, I thought, just maybe, I could find it here in the books. And I did!!!"

Griffin opened the book to the page that showed the creature, which was called a Squonk, and he turned the book around to show his grandfather. "So, what do you think, Grandpa? This is exactly what it looked like!"

Grandpa quickly pulled the chair next to Griffin. He took the book from Griffin's hands and looked at the picture. He examined it closely and read the paragraph describing the creature.

"That is rather incredible, Griffin. How did you find it again? How close did you and Caleigh get to it? Could you really see it clearly? Are you certain it wasn't a young bear? Did it see you?" Grandpa asked the questions so rapidly that Griffin didn't have a chance to get an answer in edgewise.

"So, you DO believe me? You believe we saw something? THANK YOU, Grandpa! I hoped you would believe me and now you HAVE to keep our secret. Caleigh and I don't want anything horrible to happen to it. We already saw it crying about something!"

Griffin told the story a second time, a bit more slowly and with greater detail. He didn't leave out a thing, even the part where Caleigh pretended to get sick. He described, to the best of his memory, what the strange sound was and how it drew them farther into the woods. They HAD to find the source of the sound. He closed his eyes, vividly recalling every detail of the

Squonk; short and brown with bumpy skin and fine hair all over its body. And the face, the eyes were so very sad, of course, because the creature was crying. It didn't have a mean face at all. He didn't see menacing sharp teeth or anything that would make him afraid of the creature. When he finished, Griffin looked expectantly at his grandfather.

Grandpa slowly nodded his head. "I believe you, Griffin. I completely believe that the two of you saw something you had never seen before and you were so smart staying back and just watching. Now, I can't say that it was a Squonk. These are supposed to be mythical creatures, Griffin, but who am I to say? I think it would be best, though, if the two of you did NOT look for it again."

"What?" Griffin exclaimed. "You don't think we should look for it again? Why not? If there is anything we might be able to do to make it feel better, I think we should try!"

Grandpa slouched in his chair and sighed. "I don't think so, Griffin. This creature has obviously stayed hidden and protected in our woods for a very, VERY long time. Do you want to take the chance that you might bring unwanted attention to it, just by accident? Imagine what could happen, and then the poor creature would have even more to cry about!"

Griffin listened intently to his grandfather's words. Wasn't that the reason he didn't tell his dad and the forest ranger the whole truth? He wanted to protect the creature. Griffin looked at his grandfather and smiled. "I knew you would believe me and I know you will keep my secret. I'll talk to Caleigh and we won't put the creature in any danger of being found out."

Grandpa and Griffin exchanged glances, smiles, and hugs and left the library, with his grandpa's arm draped over Griffin's shoulders.

Chapter 9: A Decision

Griffin got home from his grandparents a bit too late on Sunday night to call Caleigh. He figured he would see her in school anyway, so he went right to bed. That night, he had that same strange dream. The whole night he heard the song that they had heard in the forest, and he awoke again to a feeling of sadness. He was aware that his hand was balled up tight into a fist and when he opened it, in his palm was a tiny Caleigh.

Shaking his head awake, Griffin mumbled, "Arghhhhhhh! What does that mean?"

He pondered again whether the dream was some kind of prediction about an event in the future. He scampered out of bed, completed his morning routine, and walked thoughtfully into the kitchen. His mom was making him an egg on bagel sandwich for breakfast and already had a glass of milk sitting at his place at the table. His dad was drinking his coffee and reading the local newspaper. He lowered it when he heard Griffin sit down and said, "You and Grandpa seem to have had a rather long conversation in the library yesterday. Anything you'd like to share?"

Griffin looked up and did the best he could to maintain a calm face. "There really is nothing to share, Dad. Grandpa and I were telling stories about the funny creatures he always likes to talk about, and he actually pulled out a bunch of his books to show me where the stories came from originally. It was pretty neat that he knew all of this without having to look it up! Then, when he showed me the stories, well, it is just amazing that he has such a great memory. He never forgets a detail. We got carried away telling stories. That was all."

He waited for his dad's reaction, and when Mr. McGee smiled and agreed that his dad had an incredible memory, Griffin relaxed. "Whew, that was a bit too close," he thought.

Griffin couldn't get out the front door fast enough to meet up with Caleigh and tell her about Sunday's events while walking to school. He kissed his mom goodbye, grabbed his backpack, shouted "bye" to his dad, and bounded out the front door, jumping from the porch down to the sidewalk. Without missing a beat, he ran to the foot of Caleigh's front steps. He was just about to run up when she came flying out the front door and nearly jumped right on top of him.

"Sheesh, Griffin! I didn't see you standing there. I nearly knocked you over." Caleigh chuckled as she caught her balance, yanking her backpack up from the sidewalk and over her shoulder. "So, tell me, anything extraordinary happen at your grandparents' house yesterday?"

Griffin grabbed her arm and leaned over to whisper in her ear. "Holy cow. Did it ever! I discovered what our creature is," he hissed excitedly.

Caleigh stopped dead in her tracks and whipped her head around to stare straight into Griffin's eyes. "Tell me you are NOT lying to me, Griff. SWEAR IT!"

Griffin smiled one of the broadest smiles she had ever seen and continued to walk, pulling her along. He nodded his head rapidly and leaned over again, whispering, "It's called a Squonk. Grandpa had a book that had its picture in it AND it had a story about it too. According to the story, the Squonk cries because it is unhappy with how it looks. A hunter caught one once in a sack and when he got home, there was nothing left in the sack but a big puddle of water because the Squonk dissolved itself by crying!"

Caleigh stopped again, turned to face him straight on, and said, "You expect me to believe that? What a load of cow pies!"

Griffin was shocked that she responded that way. He was being so sincere in his explanation and he was sure that Caleigh would believe him. He reached over with both hands and grabbed each side of her face, and looking her dead in the eyes, said, "I have NEVER EVER lied to you about anything that was important, and THIS is pretty darn important. Grandpa gave me the book to bring home. It's in my room. After school, come over and I will show it to you. What is even MORE important, though, is that I told Grandpa EVERYTHING. Every single detail, and he believed me. He said we did a good thing keeping our distance and just watching. He also said he thought we should leave it alone and not try to find it again because bad stuff could happen. That's the last thing we want, of course. So, I kind of agreed not to look for it again." When he finished, he let go of her face and stepped back, waiting for her reaction.

Caleigh wrinkled her brow like she was concentrating with all her might on some huge problem she was trying to solve. Suddenly she leaped forward and gave Griffin a huge hug. "Well done, Griff! I know how great your grandpa is at keeping secrets, so for now, our Squonk is safe. I know you felt like you needed to agree with him about leaving it alone, but we can't! There is no reason for that sweet creature to feel sad about how it looks and if we can just show it we can be friends and like being with it no matter how it looks, then maybe it won't feel so sad all the time."

Griffin took a step back and shook his head slowly. "Caleigh, I can't do that! I promised my grandpa that we wouldn't try to find it again. I won't break a promise to him."

Caleigh grabbed his hand and started walking toward school. She was silent for a block or two. Then she did a quick reverse, changing hands with Griffin and walking backwards while talking softly and deliberately. "I never said that we had to go look for it. We can just let the Squonk find us! We know where we saw it last and if we just go into the general area again, well, maybe it will find us. We can have some fruits and veggies to lay out for it, kind of like an invitation to a picnic. We can even have soft music playing. Ya know, make it friendly for the Squonk. What do you think?"

By this time, they had reached the front steps of the school and Griffin stopped. He looked as seriously as he could at Caleigh and said, "We have to talk about this some more. But we can't talk about it in the open and especially not here at school. We really don't want anybody here overhearing our conversation. We just can't take that chance. So, just come over my house after school, I'll show you the book, and we can talk about your ideas then. OK?"

Caleigh nodded in agreement but in her mind, the decision was made.

Chapter 10: A Conversation

Griffin had never been in this position before. He had to make a choice between acquiescing to his best friend's wishes and breaking a promise to his beloved grandfather. Loyalty to others, even to the point of hurting himself, was central to him, and yet here he had to choose between loyalties to two people. And two people, though he would never admit this to Caleigh, that he loved. What is the right thing to do; is a promise more sacred than friendship? And added to that, what was the right thing to do about the creature — to leave it in its sadness but within its own place in nature, or to try, through trickery, to help it? And what if by helping it the creature became known to the world and was captured and displayed in a zoo? Griffin pictured that tear-stained face inside a cage and he felt a sudden rush of sickness and anxiety. As a child he was not used to the awful sense of dread that can come with being responsible for something and knowing that your choices may cause immense hurt. Griffin had also come to a decision; it was just the opposite one to his best friend's.

The meeting after school wasn't a good one. Griffin showed Caleigh his grandpa's book and read to her the story about the Squonk that had been captured by the hunter.

"You see," Caleigh had said when he had finished reading, "that story just shows how sad that poor creature is. We must be able to make its life a happier one."

Griffin had taken an entirely different message from the same story, however. "The poor Squonk would rather die, or at least dissolve, which I guess is like dying, than be trapped. Imagine if that happened because of us, and you can't say for certain that it won't, Caleigh!"

Now, the children had squabbled before — they were best friends, after all — but they had never argued about anything that really mattered. Very quickly both were swept into a whirlpool of emotion, a terrifying mix of anger and tearfulness from which it was impossible to break free. They simply were not able to listen clearly to each other.

Finally, Caleigh turned to Griffin and said, "OK, if you won't help, then I'll do it myself. Some best friend you turned out to be!"

Griffin retorted with, "Don't be silly, you can't go into the woods on your own. You'll get lost and I won't be there to help!"

"Help?" yelled Caleigh. "Remember the last time we went for a hike; we walked miles out of our way because I trusted YOU to know where you were going. I won't ever make that mistake again!" And with that she stormed home, leaving Griffin red in the face, breathing hard and struggling to not give in to his urge to cry.

Chapter 11: Now What?

Neither child slept well that night but when sleep finally claimed them, both were haunted by almost identical dreams. In these dreams, they were in the forest where they had met the Squonk but the woodland was no longer the benign place that they had entered that weekend. The woods always felt like a young place where the trees with their fresh green leaves were glad to share their light with the wildflowers that grew at their feet. But in the dreams, the woods had become a dark and somber place where the trees horded their light like misers, and where below them only ferns, brambles, and nettles could thrive with the little light that their mighty floral cousins allowed to fall between their leaves. In these dreams, the children were constantly searching, following paths that seemed at first to be full of hope but that twisted and turned until both children were hopelessly lost, cut by the brambles, and stung by nettles.

Griffin startled awake, finding himself in a puddle of sweat and breathing hard. "What a creepy dream. What can it possibly mean?" he pondered.

Slowly he got out of bed and started his normal school routine, then suddenly stopped. "I just know that Caleigh is going to do something stupid today; I KNOW IT," he muttered.

He got dressed quickly, but not in his school clothes. Instead, he pulled on the cargo shorts that he liked to wear while hiking and a long-sleeve t-shirt. "This shirt should protect my arms from all the nettles and prickly bushes," he reasoned to himself. As he got dressed, he worked on the excuse he was going to give his parents for wearing such different clothing to school. He decided upon a scavenger hunt at school; that shouldn't surprise them too much. His school always did cool things like that.

Griffin packed up his backpack and threw his camera in, just in case. One more look around his room for good measure to make sure he wasn't forgetting something important... the compass! He absolutely wanted to have the compass with him; he dare not get lost again! Oh, and the cell phone. Normally he did not take it to school, but today was different.

With that, he loped down the steps, walked into the kitchen, grabbed a piece of toast from the table and his bagged lunch from the counter, and shouted on his way out the door, "See you later! I was supposed to be at school earlier today to get ready for a scavenger hunt and I woke up late. No time to talk. Love you; see you later!"

Before anyone could say a word to him, he was out the door, down the steps, and walking rapidly to Caleigh's house. He was about to walk up her steps when Mrs. Providence stepped outside with a look of surprise.

"Griffin! I thought Caleigh was with you. She told me that you two had to leave early today to get ready for a scavenger hunt at school, so she raced out the door with a bag of food and only a muffin for breakfast."

Griffin nodded to Mrs. Providence, "That's right, but I woke up late. I kind of hoped she would wait for me. Don't worry, I'll catch up to her!"

He turned and sped down the street toward school, all the while chuckling to himself. "We are such good friends, we even come up with the same stories to tell, sheesh!"

As he reached the corner to head for school, he looked around to make sure he wasn't being watched. Then he turned to walk toward the forest instead. He knew, for sure, that Caleigh was heading into the woods to look for the Squonk, and he had a very bad feeling about it.

Chapter 12: Planning an Encounter

Caleigh walked quickly, taking all the side streets, toward the forest. She didn't want anyone to catch her "cutting" school. That would ruin all of her plans.

Before she left her house, she packed a large plastic grocery bag full of all kinds of fruits and vegetables and even some mini-muffins and cookies. She had no idea what sort of foods the Squonk might like, so she figured packing an assortment of things would be the smartest to do. She almost got caught doing that when her mother walked in on her. "Stuff for today's scavenger hunt," she blurted out. "Griff and I were assigned to bring food things for the hunt. I have to meet him in a couple minutes 'cause we volunteered to go in early to help Mrs. Mitchell get things ready to hide."

She couldn't believe she came up with that on the spur of the moment and hoped that Griffin would NOT come to her house this morning and ruin it all.

Caleigh walked the two-mile distance to the forest entrance quickly, deep in thought. She was going to locate the spot they marked where they had seen the Squonk. She had a good sense of direction and completely remembered the path they took on Rimrock

Trail. She wanted to look around the area a bit more. After all, she and Griff stayed completely hidden when they saw the Squonk and didn't take any time to truly scout out the clearing. The Squonk seemed to just disappear into the tall leaves, but that was quite impossible.

"There must be tons of hiding places all around the clearing and I want to find the ones that might be the most secure for my new Squonk friend," Caleigh murmured out loud. She continued to plan... once she found some good hiding places, she would put some treats out for the Squonk and just sit back very quietly and watch. If it did come out for something, then she would decide how to approach it, to show she meant no harm and was a friend.

It took her about 25 minutes to get to the trail entrance. Caleigh stopped, looked around, took a deep breath and said, "This is it. I AM going to show the Squonk that I CAN be a friend!"

Chapter 13: Seeking the Squonk

Caleigh practically skipped with glee onto the trail. She was truly excited with her plan. First, she would make sure she was comfortable with the area where they spotted the Squonk. Then, she would try to figure out where it might hide to be safe and away from prying eyes. For a split second she stopped walking and thought about that last task — finding where it could stay safe away from prying eyes. "Hmmmmm, wasn't that kind of exactly what Griffin was talking about?" she mused. She remembered that he was worried that too many people could find out about the Squonk and that would harm it. She certainly didn't want to harm it, but wanted it to understand that it didn't need to be sad and it could have friends.

"Isn't that worth the effort?" she said aloud. "Yes, yes, it is worth it!" she convinced herself.

When she approached the split on the trail, she remembered the coin toss and that she and Griffin took the path on the right, following the stream. "That turkey even made a race out of it," she laughed to herself.

She continued down the path, taking in all the usual beauty of the forest surrounding her. The autumn trees were starting to change colors but most were still a brilliant green and full of leaves. Sunlight streaked through the high branches and washed the ferns and soft pink mountain laurels in a gentle glow. Caleigh smiled as she closed her eyes and faced the sky, the warmth of the sunbathing her face with a gentle light. She slowly hugged herself and turned in a circle, whispering, "I just love standing in the middle of the forest; I love the smells, the sounds, and the colors. This really is my happy place! I bet that's why it's the Squonk's happy place too."

She moved deeper into the woods, watching for the spot where they had left the main trail to get to the pond. "I wish I had asked Griffin to make me a copy of those pictures he took," she grumbled aloud. "That would make this so much easier! Then again, if I did, he would know I was going back to the secret Squonk spot. Got to do this one on my own."

With renewed determination, she scanned the area for something familiar. After a few minutes, Caleigh spotted it. About five feet away was a huge tree trunk that had an enormous burl on the side. "There you are, my little navigation guide... glad to see you!"

Caleigh knew that exact tree was where they left the main trail to follow the sounds they heard, so off she went past the tree, onto the smaller path, heading toward the next landmark she hoped to find on her way to the pond. She walked along the narrow trail, humming softly to herself, completely unaware that she was being followed. As she hiked toward the pond, Caleigh reviewed her plan out loud. She always thought more clearly when she said things out loud.

"OK. The first thing I have to do is find an area where I KNOW that the Squonk will be safe; at least, it can't be easily seen from any trails. Next, I will set up a comfortable place for it to sit and munch on the treats I have for it. I will want to be close by so it can see me and see that I am not going to hurt it."

She continued walking, spotting each of the landmarks Griffin had taken pictures of, more assured with each step that she was getting closer to the pond. Then she suddenly stopped.

"What is wrong with me? How can I be so rude and call the Squonk 'IT' all this time? IT? Nothing would be friends with you if you only called it 'IT'! I wonder if the Squonk is a boy or girl or what?? Is the Squonk like some giant amoeba creature? Before I meet the creature again, I have to figure out a name!"

With an additional goal on her mind, Caleigh moved deeper into the woods, watching for the clearing and still unaware of the stealthy movement behind her.

Chapter 14: The Backup

Griffin was trying to figure out how much earlier Caleigh had left her house. Her mom really did not let on how much time had passed, just that she had left earlier. Griffin picked up his pace, almost breaking into a jog. He didn't want to attract attention. The last thing he wanted was to be caught by a police officer and turned in to the school principal, or even worse, to his parents for cutting school.

He looked at his watch; it was still early, only 8:15, but he just knew that Caleigh had started so much earlier that she had to be well along the path back into the deeper part of the forest. "How is she going to find her way without my pictures? I know she has a great memory, but we made some tricky turns. Arrrrrgggggghhhhh! She is so frustrating!" Griffin fumed... and worried... and walked faster.

Finally, he reached the entrance of the park and went directly to the trailhead; Rimrock felt foreboding today, and Griffin didn't like it. He moved forward quickly, remembered that they had flipped the coin and turned right at the fork, and proceeded down the trail at a fairly rapid speed. Griffin envisioned them running along this path until they came to the creaky old bridge. "Ah, there it is," he exclaimed. Relieved to reach it, he gingerly crept across, then reverted to his fast, focused pace through the forest. He was glad he remembered the camera that had the trail marker pictures on it; his memory wasn't nearly as good as Caleigh's. As he moved deeper into the forest, he turned his camera on to look for some of the trail markers.

"Where was that first turn?" he wondered. He looked at the pictures and saw the tree with the big bump on it.

"THAT'S where we turned to the smaller trail!" Griffin stopped walking and began scanning the forest area for that tree. It felt like forever until he finally spotted it, but there it was and there was the narrow trail. He turned down that path and thought he should try calling out Caleigh's name. He hoped she would be nice and return his shout if she heard him and not ignore him if she was still angry.

"Caleigh! Caaaaaaaaaleigh!" Griffin yelled her name as loudly as he could.

Nothing.

He was getting more nervous by the minute as he kept following the path toward the pond.

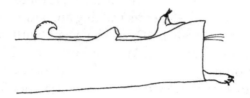

Chapter 15: A Long Way Down

Meanwhile, Caleigh remembered all of the navigation spots and found the pond fairly quickly. She located the pink granite stone, lifted it, and found Griffin's magnifying glass and her Alice in Wonderland figurine.

Caleigh hooted with glee. "This is the exact spot! EXCELLENT!" She gently laid the stone back in place.

She set about scouting the area for a perfect place to set up the food gifts she had brought the Squonk. Caleigh wondered if the Squonk would venture back to the pond, thought about that for a minute, and decided that it might not, so she would follow its path through the ferns.

Green eyes followed her every move.

Caleigh headed in the last direction she and Griffin had seen the Squonk go and peered around to get a feeling for where she was going now. This was foreign territory; neither she nor Griffin had been here before so she didn't know what to expect. If it was possible, this part of the forest seemed even more filled with tall trees, ferns, moss and lichen-covered logs and tiny flowers.

"Amazing!" she exclaimed out loud.

Looking around in awe, Caleigh forgot to pay attention to where she was walking and stumbled over a fallen tree branch. Over she went with a thud, twisting her ankle. "YEOW, that hurts," she bellowed. She got on her knees to steady herself, trying to stand to see how much weight she could put on her foot and came face-to-face with a Pennsylvania bobcat!

Caleigh could barely breathe. She was terrified. She had nothing to protect herself with and even though she knew that bobcats were not deadly to people, as mountain lions or bears were, they had huge teeth and were wild animals. The bobcat stood and stared at Caleigh, measuring her every move.

"What to do, what to do????" Caleigh never imagined anything like this would ever happen and she had no plan. She knew her ankle hurt, and she also knew she could not remain in a stare-down with this animal.

"I have got to find some way to move from here and get to a spot where someone can find me," she thought. With that in mind, Caleigh slowly struggled to her feet, not taking her eyes off the bobcat. She began to cautiously back away from the animal, continuing to maintain eye contact the entire time. But the bobcat studiously followed her. Fear overwhelmed Caleigh. Tears slipped down her cheeks and she turned to run.

"HELP!" she screamed as loud as she could while running as quickly as she could on her injured ankle. She felt like she was truly running for her life. The bobcat slinked after her, following but not attacking.

Caleigh had absolutely no idea where she was in the forest now and ran in any random direction. She crashed through some thick ferns to find that nothing was there in front of her but sky! She tumbled down a hillside of loose stones into a deep gully. It was too steep and the stones too loose for her to climb out. Caleigh was stuck!

She sat there, in shock, looking toward the top of the hill where the bobcat simply peered down at her.

As she silently cried, trying to figure out what to do now, another pair of eyes was watching her very intently.

Chapter 16: A Wailing Cry

Caleigh took several deep breaths to try to calm herself and stem the tears. She was more frightened than she had ever been in her entire life. She kept looking around to see if there was any possible hidden path that would allow her to climb out of the gully, but there was nothing except more gravel. Her ankle was killing her; Caleigh worried that it might actually be broken.

She periodically looked toward the top of the hillside to see if she could still see the bobcat. There it was, looking down, observing her.

After 30 minutes or so, Caleigh began to hope that Griffin would come looking for her. She knew that he was very upset with her plan, totally disagreeing with her, and that he would be really angry when he got to school and discovered that she was absent. "Maybe he will get brave at lunchtime and leave to look for me," she said out loud to nobody in particular. "At least, I hope so."

Caleigh decided it might be a good idea to lie down and try to take a nap. She could put her foot up; she remembered from her first aid class that elevating an injured body part helped stop swelling. So she pushed the sharp chunks of gravel aside and found some softer earth underneath. "That will be perfect for a quick nap."

She dug out a little soft bed area, used the excavated materials to elevate her foot, and then used her backpack as a pillow. She laid down, gingerly lifting her ankle up on the mound of dirt and rocks, and whimpered herself to sleep.

As she slept, the hidden glowing eyes moved toward the bobcat. A small mouse suddenly appeared out of nowhere at the cat's feet and he gobbled it up. He started to sniff around for more game; he had become hungry watching the creature that had fallen into the gully. Another mouse! And then another! The bewildered bobcat had no idea that he was being baited away from Caleigh. By the fourth mouse, the bobcat was several hundred feet back into the forest and ran off in search of some different food.

Glowing golden eyes quickly moved back to the gully and looked down to see if Caleigh was still there. She was.

The Squonk wailed very softly. He felt so badly. "That poor creature is hurt and can't get back to the top of this hill." The Squonk recognized Caleigh from her visit to Rimrock the week before. He remembered that she had a friend with her. He wondered where the friend was now. Slowly, Squonk took tiny steps down the hillside, moving so carefully that the loose stones didn't shift under his feet. He moved cautiously, not sure how the creature would respond to him. It seemed to be sleeping. That was good. At least it wasn't crying any more. The Squonk felt terrible to see the creature cry; it made him want to cry too. Once Squonk reached Caleigh, he slowly bent down to see if she would move.

Nothing. Creature was sleeping soundly.

"Good! I can help creature get more comfortable and stay warm just in case nobody comes to help soon," thought Squonk. He softly and quietly began to gather fallen leaves. Even though they were crunchy, they would still keep things comfortable for Creature. After collecting several mounds of leaves, he gingerly placed them all around the Creature, blanketing her with warmth.

He cocked his head to the side, gazing with great curiosity. He remembered from the last time that the Creature and friend were quiet and gentle. They didn't make loud sounds or try to catch him like so many others in the woods had. He also remembered the little sounds of surprise that they both made when they saw him. Squonk was used to those kinds of creatures making very loud noises and running toward him from the forest whenever they spotted him. "That is always so scary!" he thought.

The very memory of the other creatures yelling and pointing fingers and running toward him made him feel sad and for an instant, he wailed. The low soft wail, songlike, drifted lightly through the air. Caleigh's eyes fluttered sleepily at the familiar sound.

Chapter 17: The Meeting

Griffin was racing as fast as his legs could carry him toward the clearing. As he descended the path, he could not contain his anger at his friend, even moreso because he was also afraid for her. What do you do if someone does the opposite of what you want her to do? If Caleigh had been a boy, they might have ended up wrestling.

"Hmmm, would be a good result," Griffin thought. He was rather good at wrestling and he was sure he could pin her down and, in that way, prove that after all he was right. If he was her parent, he could stop her allowance or ground her, but since she was a girl and his own age, he would just have to argue with her — Griffin had to admit Caleigh was rather good with words.

The path narrowed further, and brambles that curled their way among the tree trunks caught at his bare legs, leaving little red stinging trails across his skin. Despite it being morning, the dark, full, late-summer foliage made the wood feel like a dark place. There were no sounds of birds; instead, the silence was broken only by the sound of some distant branch breaking. He hoped he was going in the right direction but even with his camera as a record it was so hard to be sure. One path looked just like another when they entwined their way through the forest.

In his mind, as he walked, he imagined various scenarios for his friend, the best of which always involved Caleigh being stuck in a predicament that would involve Griffin having to come to the rescue, while he fought valiantly with his own urge to tell her that he had told her so. And then the thought occurred to him that maybe the Squonk wasn't a kind creature at all and had planned this all along in order to capture one of them. What if, despite its size, tears, and warty appearance, it was a fierce and very wild beast?

Griffin bellowed "Caleigh!" again but much louder, as much to reassure himself that he was doing the right thing as to locate his missing friend. There was no answer, just another distant crack of a branch.

What if the Squonk had captured Caleigh and was now stalking him? Was it the Squonk making its way through the forest that was creating the sounds that he was hearing? Griffin's breathing quickened and he looked around nervously, but a seemingly infinite procession of trees blocked his view.

And then there was another cracking sound in the trees behind him. In sheer panic he started to run deeper into the woods, stumbling, falling, ignoring the brambles and the nettles as they continued to tear against him, his breaths coming in great gasps as he headed further and further into the forest. Griffith began wishing that there was someone to protect him, an adult to keep him safe.

Why had he and Caleigh been so foolish as to think that they could figure this out themselves? He watched closely for every picture clue as he sped through the brush, trying to make all the correct turns. Finally he noticed what seemed to be a light at the end of the path. Light must mean an escape from this uncomfortable dark forest, to safety. With even greater speed, Griffin headed toward the light. The trees began to thin out and he darted out into a clearing where he found the pond. He instantly spotted the pink rock that marked the spot and sat down next to it, trying to think like Caleigh.

"What would she do next?" he pondered out loud. He stood and scanned the area and it came to him. She would head in the last direction that they saw the Squonk disappear and try to find it that way. He turned very slowly, trying to remember the exact location, and then he saw it! Caleigh had dropped one of her scavenger-hunt food items exactly where he thought the tiny path taken by the creature was located.

"Thank you, Caleigh! Whether you knew you did this or not, thank you!"

The thought of re-entering the forest made his heartbeat with a faster, more powerful rhythm again, but he was here now and he couldn't return without Caleigh. He started down the small path, and this time he watched every step so that he could follow her footsteps as closely as possible. It felt like he was walking for miles when he heard a rustling in the brush. He stopped and listened; it was like a plaintive cry but it was wordless. He listened again, and there, just above the gentlest of sounds that the human ear can sense, he heard it again: a song without words but with a melody that sounded so sad. Could it be Caleigh? He tried to orient himself to where the sound was coming from and then pushed his way through the grass toward where it seemed to originate.

"Caleigh?" he called out.

Nothing.

He had to try again. "CALEIGH!" he called out a bit louder.

Suddenly, like a bolt out of the blue, a large cat leaped across the path in front of him and pounced on what appeared to be some sort of prey.

"WHOA!!!" Griffin screamed out in fright. He looked around to try to see what exactly had just jumped in front of him, but then his good sense made him realize that he probably shouldn't be hanging around wild animals. And with that, he took off running, again trying to follow what looked like Caleigh's path.

At this point his heart was pounding even harder with fear, and his imagination was running wild. What if that thing attacked Caleigh? What if it bit her? What if it thought SHE was some kind of prey?

Griffin was now running headlong into the same dense bushes that Caleigh had entered. He stopped suddenly when he heard the sound again. The song was louder now; he was clearly heading in the right direction. It was coming from just ahead of where he was standing.

As he moved cautiously toward the sound, he realized that moving slowly was a good idea, because there, right in front of him, was a sudden drop-off down into a deep gully. As he stopped and looked down, he could not believe his eyes. Standing right by Caleigh's side, softly wailing, was the Squonk!

Griffin held his breath. He didn't know what to think or what to do. Was it being friendly? Was it just curiously looking her over? Was Caleigh asleep or unconscious? Was she hurt? As he watched, the Squonk gently placed more leaves around her, like he was making some sort of bed for her, and then he picked up her hand and held it in his, again wailing softly.

Griffin's heart began to race again. He accidentally dislodged a stone and it fell into the gully, knocking other stones in its path downwards. As each stone tumbled and fell, the sound echoed up from the gully. The creature looked up to see what had made the sound. He saw Griffin. The Squonk's eyes were huge, set in its warty skin, and its hand was now on Caleigh's shoulder.

A gut-wrenching mix of emotions — a bit of anger and mostly fear — filled Griffin. He picked up a stone from the top of the ravine, poised, ready to throw. His eyes met the creature's eyes and despite the anger that was written all over Griffin's face, the Squonk's golden brown eyes gently returned his gaze. The Squonk's expression was remarkably calm and friendly. Then the most unexpected thing happened. The Squonk seemed to smile and lifted its other arm, making a "come down" motion, and in Griffin's mind the creature spoke! Its voice sounded as if it was the wind gently stirring the grasses, not loud, but surprisingly clear and without a note of fear in it.

"Your friend is hurt; I am helping her. Please, come down to help!"

Griffin's heart was beating wildly; the stone was still in his hand, his mind racing. The creature held his gaze but not in an aggressive way and telepathically spoke again. "Perhaps we can both help her?"

Griffin didn't say a word but quickly dropped the stone in his hand. He looked again at Caleigh and the creature and now understood the scene before him. The Squonk's hand was still on his friend's shoulder but rather than looking as if it was grasping her, it now looked protective. Griffin's breathing began to still, and as he calmed down, he hoped the Squonk might just be the adult that he had wished would come to their aid. As he looked into the huge eyes for reassurance, questions tumbled through his head like the autumn leaves.

"How am I going to get down there safely? How did he get down there without getting hurt? How am I going to get her out of there?"

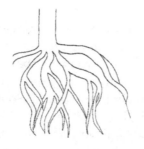

Chapter 18: The Rescue

When you are afraid and high above a steep drop, all routes down look equally terrifying. Griffin could see no safe way down to Caleigh from where he was, and he looked to the Squonk for some form of direction. The Squonk again met his gaze and as it did, words formed in Griffin's mind. It was not his own voice that he heard, but a gentle and melodious one instead. The voice pointed out a tree root that emerged from the rocks in the gully, which led down toward where Caleigh was lying.

"Breathe, breathe deeply. You can do this and I will guide you," the voice said.

Griffin did as he was bid and shuffled on his bottom to where the tree root protruded the most. The root was gnarled, but it was alive and looked strong. In places it split into two and then the separate roots tangled together, making a series of steps like a ladder leading to the floor of the gully. Griffin clung to the root with one hand and then dangled his feet until they found a secure foothold within the tree's root system. Again and again, he breathed deeply and without looking down he used his sense of touch to guide himself downwards.

The voice continued to encourage him, telling him how well he was doing and as it did, he gained confidence and his movements became less timid. He summoned the courage to look down and saw that he was close to the bottom and the Squonk's warty hand was outstretched to catch his. In three more steps he could jump and land within some fallen leaves and soft sand that had itself slid down the slope. Griffin swiftly clambered down the last steps of his natural ladder and jumped. The Squonk's hand grasped his, and Griffin landed close to Caleigh's side. The Squonk squeezed his hand and smiled. Once Griffin had regained his breath, he returned the gesture and smile.

Caleigh, who was lying beside them both, opened her eyes with a sharp intake of breath, as the pain in her ankle returned. "Griffin! You came for me!" she said with relief.

And then she turned to see the Squonk, but before she could say anything, Griffin said, "It's OK, Caleigh; the Squonk looked after you the whole time and he helped me too."

He looked around toward the area and said, "But I don't know how we get out from here; I can't carry you up the way that I got down to you and everywhere else there is a steep slope."

"See if you can help me up on my feet, Griff," Caleigh responded. Both children tried but Griffin couldn't support Caleigh on his own.

A voice formed in both of their minds. "I can help too, if you don't mind." The children looked to the Squonk and nodded. Caleigh grabbed her backpack and Squonk gently took Caleigh's other arm over his shoulder. The three of them began to walk together, a single step at a time.

"But how can we escape from here?" Caleigh asked. The Squonk pointed to a patch of ferns growing in the deepest part of the gully. The three of them made their way toward the ferns. When they reached the tall plants, the Squonk parted them, and Caleigh and Griffin could see that hidden behind was a shallow cave. At the end of the cave, a light seemed to lead out into the forest again.

The three stepped carefully through the ferns and, supporting Caleigh, hobbled into the entrance of the cave. The cave itself was softly illuminated with the light of what looked to be candles. But most remarkably, the walls of the cave were painted with beautiful depictions of the creatures of the forest. There was the bobcat, its jaws agape, ready to pounce. There were deer emerging in a clearing of the forest and even a copper-colored snake swimming in one of the pools. As they walked further through the cave, the animal pictures changed to include some that were no longer found in the forest, like wolves, and then there, in the center of the cave, were two paintings that dwarfed all the rest. One was a gigantic russet-colored mammoth, its tusks and trunk raised as it gave out a bellow of challenge. Close by was another image of a cat, but this cat was far bigger than the bobcat and its teeth were like blades; sheltered beside it were its kittens, snuggling in for warmth and protection.

The paintings were exquisite and despite her pain Caleigh said to the Squonk, "These are so beautiful — who painted them?"

The Squonk lowered its head shyly, making it clear that the artist was the Squonk itself.

How?! How could it have painted creatures that had been extinct for many thousands of years? That thought crossed both Caleigh and Griffin's minds at the same time; maybe, just maybe, somehow the Squonk had seen them too.

"How old are you?" Griffin and Caleigh asked simultaneously.

Squonk's answer glided through their minds, and Griffin and Caleigh saw great plains of grass, with a gigantic mammoth ploughing through the long grass as if it was a ship crossing an ocean. Then, on a granite pillar towering above the grass sat the saber-toothed cat gently washing its kittens.

Slowly the scene changed as saplings grew in the grasses, and they seemed to march across the plains, sprouting up like a conquering army. As they moved steadily forward, they grew taller and taller until the grassland was gone and the land became a forest. Within the forest, streams flowed and glades formed. Griffin and Caleigh could hear the sounds of all the living things that had made the forest their own. Now a wolf stood on the granite tower that had once been the castle of the saber-toothed cat and howled its greeting to the pack that rested below. A bear delicately picked fruit from the trees with its claws, feasting on nature's gifts.

The scene changed again, and the children saw the forest creatures of now. Then for one brief moment a human appeared between the trees, its eyes searching, but for what? The vision finished and the children were now at the exit of the cave. They looked at each other with amazement.

"Could the Squonk REALLY be that old? What next?" they both thought.

Chapter 19: A Secret Promise

Outside the cave, the Squonk continued to help them find their way back to the clearing where they had first seen him and unbeknownst to them, the Squonk had seen them too. Caleigh and Griffin turned to face their hero, for that was exactly what the Squonk now was to them: a hero for saving them both from a serious and dangerous situation.

Caleigh was the first to reach out her hand to touch the Squonk's face very gently. Stroking its cheek, she looked deep into its eyes and spoke softly from the heart. "Thank you, my friend. I came to look for you to be your friend and to see if others might also be friends with you. I didn't want you to be sad! I understand now how much you care about all living things around you and how important you are to this forest. You saved me even though I was only thinking about how to find you. I promise you, with all my heart, that you will always be a secret. I will never ever tell anyone about you, so that you can stay safe in your home here."

Then she hugged the Squonk who hugged her back and smiled a beautiful, warty, sincere smile.

As Caleigh stepped back, it was Griffin's turn. He was at a loss for words. Right in front of his eyes was one of his grandpa's incredible mythical creatures, in the flesh. This wonderful being had put all thoughts of personal danger aside to help him rescue his best friend. What can you say?

With the most gracious smile spread across his face, he walked up to the Squonk and gave him the most enormous hug that he could muster. "Thank you, thank you, thank you, Mister Squonk. We would have been lost without you and your help, and as Caleigh said, you and your home will be a permanent secret between us. We WILL keep you safe, no matter what. And I hope that maybe one day, when Caleigh and I are hiking here again, we can visit if you'd like to see us."

Griffin started to back up and the Squonk took his hand one last time, gave it a squeeze, and smiled. He nodded his head and then disappeared into the heavily ferned path behind him. Gone.

Rimrock
Hiking Trail

Epilogue: Seven Months Later

The punishment for both Caleigh and Griffin was swift and long. Both were forbidden from hiking the ANF until after the spring thaw. This was truly the worst possible consequence for them cutting school, for being dishonest (because really, they were — telling their parents that they were going on a school scavenger hunt when they weren't), and for being irresponsible after they had promised Mr. McGee and Mr. Oakes, the ANF ranger, that they would be more careful when they went into the forest.

It was late April; the snows had melted and wildflowers were emerging within the forest, each calling to the bees to come and choose them for pollination through the language of their scent and color and size of their petals. Caleigh and Griffin met at Griffin's house to create a plan to persuade their parents to let them return to the forest after their long winter exile. As they sat in Griffin's room and discussed their shared adventures, Griffin reached into his desk and produced a leather-bound notebook in which he had drawn, in exquisite detail, some of the scenes.

"I wonder, will we ever have such a fantastic adventure again?" Caleigh said, and Griffin ruefully replied, "I hope so."

And then, as if to reply to them both, the room began to fill with a gentle glowing light and an insistent and rhythmic hum. The orb, which had been both silent and dark, was returning to life. "That's strange. It hasn't glowed for months now!" exclaimed Griffin. They approached the corner of his desk to take a closer look at the orb. Both were once again startled by the scene that unfolded before them. As if on a glider, they soared past tall pillars that looked like stone archways in a huge circle, then swooped up in the sky and angled downward across great wide-open moorlands. Far in the distance emerged a huge castle. As the image in the orb slowly faded, Caleigh and Griffin faced each other and shook their heads, smiling at the thought of another brilliant adventure. But first, they had to return to their beloved forest.

Griffin and Caleigh asked permission to head back to Rimrock Trail to go on another hike. Both sets of parents reluctantly gave permission for them to go, but not before several promises were made:

DO NOT go anywhere near where Caleigh slipped down the gully.

DO NOT spend more than two hours hiking.

DO NOT go searching after strange sounds they might hear.

Caleigh and Griffin quickly and graciously made their promises. They had missed hiking so much that they were willing to promise just about anything to be able to do it again. They met on the sidewalk outside their houses; checked to make sure they had the cell phone, camera, compass, and a snack; and off they went on their first adventure in a very long time.

As soon as they got far away from all the houses, they started to talk a little bit about what they might find. "Do you think there is any chance that once we get onto Rimrock, he will find us?" asked Caleigh.

"I think he will be very careful before he shows himself to us again. It has been a long time since we were on the trail and he might not remember us," Griffin responded sullenly.

Caleigh nodded in understanding. "Oh, I hope Squonk does remember us; it would be so nice to see him again."

They finally arrived at Rimrock trailhead and immediately went onto the trails that would take them back toward the cave. Caleigh was astounded that Griffin remembered every single detail of the trails past the clearing. "He must have been really focused while Squonk was bringing us back to the clearing," she thought. "I'm so glad Griff does remember; maybe Squonk will find us again!"

In under an hour of hiking Griffin found the entrance to the cave. "Well, what do you think? Should we go in?"

Caleigh nodded enthusiastically. "Yes, please!!!"

Griffin reached into his backpack and got out his flashlight, turned it on, and they slowly entered the cave. It was darker than they remembered. Griffin moved his flashlight along the path to make sure they wouldn't trip over anything. After a few minutes he moved the light up toward the cave walls to see if they could spot the cave drawings again.

Caleigh and Griffin stopped dead in their tracks! A beautiful new drawing had appeared. There, on the wall in front of them, was a drawing of a girl and boy walking arm-in-arm with Squonk along a path in the forest! Caleigh and Griffin's faces broke into huge grins.

Squonk remembered them, FOREVER.

About the Authors

Diane Klein is a retired speech/language pathologist and professor of Deaf Education. She lives in Pittsburgh, Pennsylvania, with her husband and two kitties. She loves travel (has hit four of five continents so far and is scheduled to visit the Antarctic), adventuring (white water rafting, skydiving, hot air ballooning), reading, and spending quality time with friends and family. During those times, many stories were shared, and serendipitously, Diane met Tim, who also loved to create stories. Tossing about tales happily resulted in a transatlantic writing foray into the world of children's literature. Diane is the author of two textbooks in the field of Deaf Education but considers her greatest writing accomplishment the completion of The Mystery of the Wailing Woods. The book won rave reviews from her granddaughter, the most important critic of them all! Diane hopes you enjoy it as well.

Tim Knight grew up in Surrey in southeast England, which is a landscape like Tolkien's Shire, with its little streams, woods, and gentle rolling hills. His most formative experience was exploring this countryside with his mum. As they walked, they would create stories about the places that they visited. At school, he was what was called a "late bloomer," going from being educationally somewhat away with the fairies to studying chemistry at Imperial College in London. Coming from a large coed high school, he found the rigors of a mainly male, hardworking, and rather puritanical college tough at first. But it, and an emotional break-up, led to his finding his creative, artistic side. After graduation, Tim worked for six years as a teacher in Leicester before moving to Cornwall in 1990. Within weeks of moving there, he knew that he had returned home. Tim found his muse within its remote moorland and beaches. Writing with Diane, Tim feels as if he has been transported back fifty years, creating stories of mythical beasts that are there to be found by those who are prepared to explore just that little bit further.